Berry Magic

WRITTEN BY

Teri Sloat and Betty Huffmon

ILLUSTRATED BY

Teri Sloat

ALASKA NORTHWEST BOOKS®

Anchorage ■ Portland

Long ago,

before your grandmother's memory,

before the salmonberries and raspberries,

before the cranberries and blueberries,

there were only little black crowberries on the tundra.

They grew like dots on the tops of the hills.

Every fall, the old women grumbled about the crowberries:

"These berries are so dry."

"These berries have no taste."

"These berries are not even worth picking!"

But they picked them anyway, for there had to be *akutaq*

(uh-GOO-tuk), Eskimo ice cream, at the fall feast,

and it had to be filled with berries.

Anana (un-NAH-na) watched the old women. She liked the way their brightly trimmed *qaspeqs* (KUS-puks) decorated the tundra. And while she watched them, a plan grew in her mind.

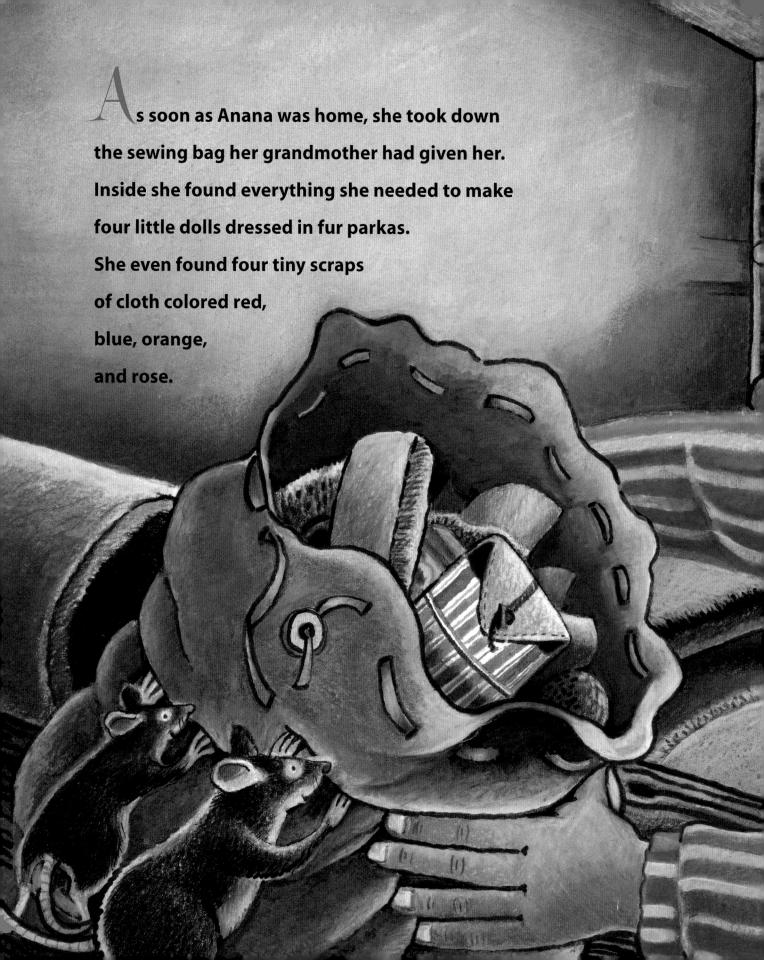

As soon as Anana was home, she took down
the sewing bag her grandmother had given her.
Inside she found everything she needed to make
four little dolls dressed in fur parkas.
She even found four tiny scraps
of cloth colored red,
blue, orange,
and rose.

She made the first doll quickly, stuffing it with dry grass. After stitching pieces of squirrel skin together for its parka, she tied the piece of red cloth around its head for a *pelatuuk* (BLAH-dook).

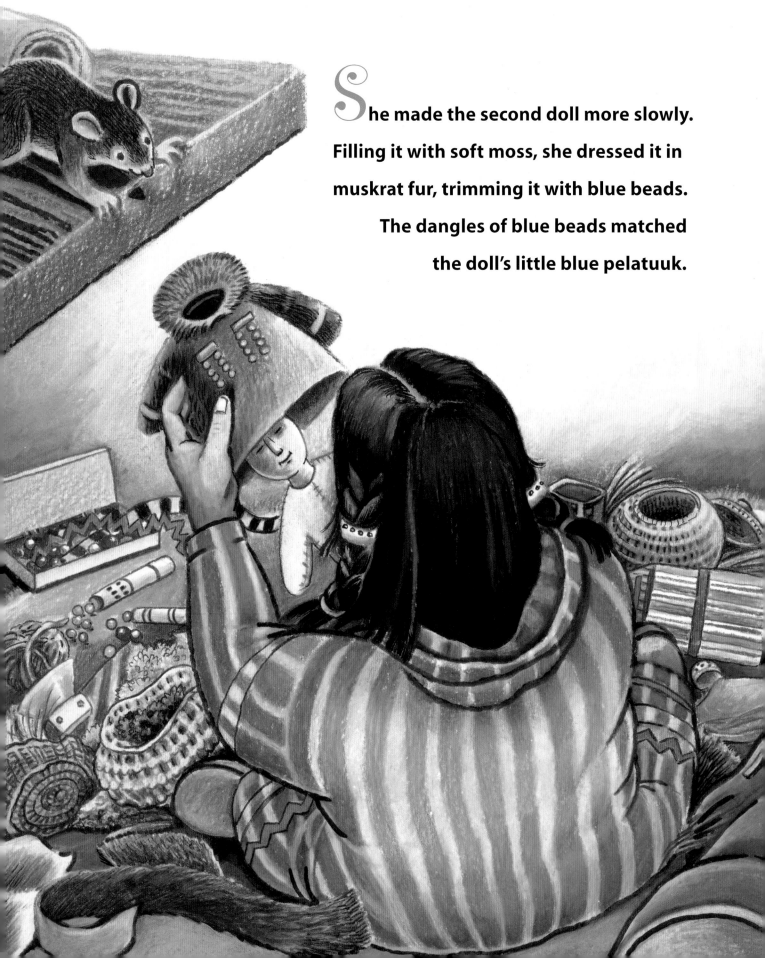

She made the second doll more slowly.
Filling it with soft moss, she dressed it in
muskrat fur, trimming it with blue beads.
The dangles of blue beads matched
the doll's little blue pelatuuk.

Anana made the third doll carefully. Filling it with
reindeer hair, she dressed it in a parka of fine reindeer
skin. She placed the doll in the window, letting the setting
sun paint an orange glow on its cheeks that matched the
pelatuuk tied around its head.

Anana made the last doll with much joy. She lovingly filled it with goose down, covered its plump body with warm fox skin, and stitched together a tiny pair of sealskin *mukluks* (MUK-luks) for its feet. Finally, she strung a necklace of rosy beads around its neck to match its pelatuuk.

She looked at her dolls and slowly drew in her breath. *"Aaaaaa-ling!"* she murmured, for she was pleased.

Then Anana wrapped the dolls in her fancy parka,
placing them inside her reindeer-skin bag,
along with her dance fans.

When the moon began to rise,
she carried the bag up a nearby hill.
With every step, her load became heavier.

At last Anana reached the crowberries at the top of the hill. She turned in a circle and looked out all around her at the vast, moonlit tundra.

When it was time, she untied her bag
and slipped the parka over her head.

Then Anana began to dance. Snuggling the ruff around her face, she sang:

"Atsa-ii-yaa (Berry)
Atsa-ii-yaa (Berry)
Átsaukina!" (Be a berry!)

Anana peeked down at her bag. Out wiggled a little girl dressed in squirrel skins and wearing a bright red pelatuuk.

The girl went tumbling down the hill, past the crowberries, leaving dots of tasty, red cranberries shining in the moonlight. Anana sang again.

"Atsa-ii-yaa Atsa-ii-yaa Átsaukina!"

Out of the bag skipped another little girl with blue beads dangling from her muskrat parka, and she wore a blue pelatuuk. While Anana danced, the girl leaped over the crowberries and past the cranberries. She rolled head-over-heels through the bushes below, leaving clusters of juicy blueberries wherever she went.

Anana danced faster, singing louder:

"Atsa-ii-yaa Atsa-ii-yaa

A happy girl, dressed in reindeer skins and wearing an orange pelatuuk, popped from the bag. She jumped over the crowberries, sprang over the cranberries, and bounced over the blueberries. She hopped across the boggy grass, from hummock to hummock, leaving a trail of tangy salmonberries on long stems.

Átsaukina!"

Knowing there was still one doll left in the bag, Anana shouted with excitement: "Atsa-ii-yaa!"

But she was too loud and the last little girl was shy. Anana lowered her voice a bit and called: "Atsa-ii-yaa!"

But the last little girl was still too shy, so Anana whispered in her kindest voice: "Átsaukina!"

The plump little girl blushed and smiled at Anana as she peeked out from the bag. With her rosy beads flying, she gave a great leap . . .

. . . beyond the crowberries
and the cranberries,
. . . beyond the blueberries
and the salmonberries,
. . . and into the grass at
the bottom of
the hill.

While Anana finished her dance, **SWEET ROSY RASPBERRIES** peeked out from the shadows.

Anana's heart was overflowing with joy as she hurried home.
While the moon was still shining, berries spread from hill to hill.
By morning, the tundra was covered with red, blue, orange,
and rosy berries. Anana woke early and filled
her baskets with berries for
the fall feast.

That night, the old women couldn't get enough of the berry-filled akutaq. While Anana danced, she heard them saying:

"These berries are so juicy!"

"These berries are so tasty!"

"Aa-ling! These berries are like magic!"

Even the grumpiest woman was smiling. Anana smiled, too.

And from that day until now, Anana's berries have filled the akutaq at every fall festival.

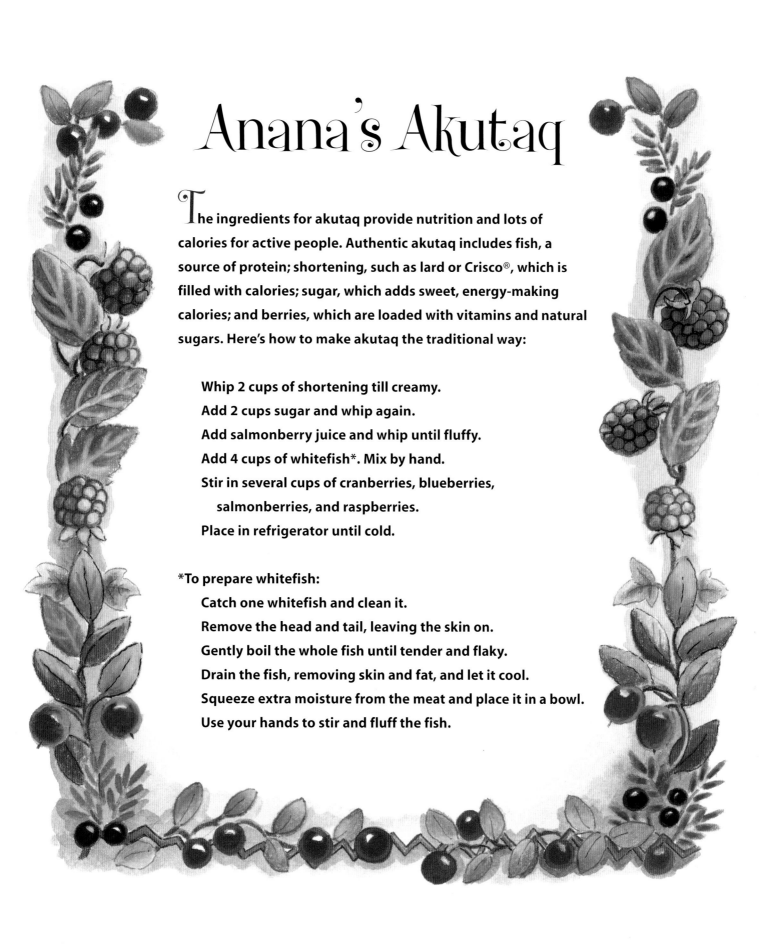

Anana's Akutaq

The ingredients for akutaq provide nutrition and lots of calories for active people. Authentic akutaq includes fish, a source of protein; shortening, such as lard or Crisco®, which is filled with calories; sugar, which adds sweet, energy-making calories; and berries, which are loaded with vitamins and natural sugars. Here's how to make akutaq the traditional way:

> Whip 2 cups of shortening till creamy.
> Add 2 cups sugar and whip again.
> Add salmonberry juice and whip until fluffy.
> Add 4 cups of whitefish*. Mix by hand.
> Stir in several cups of cranberries, blueberries,
>   salmonberries, and raspberries.
> Place in refrigerator until cold.

*To prepare whitefish:
> Catch one whitefish and clean it.
> Remove the head and tail, leaving the skin on.
> Gently boil the whole fish until tender and flaky.
> Drain the fish, removing skin and fat, and let it cool.
> Squeeze extra moisture from the meat and place it in a bowl.
> Use your hands to stir and fluff the fish.

To Betty and Helen, with love. —T. S.

A story from my past dedicated
to our future. —B.H.

Text © 2004
by Teri Sloat and Betty Huffmon
Illustrations © 2004 by Teri Sloat
Crisco is a registered trademark of The J. M. Smucker Co.

Library of Congress Cataloging-in-Publication Data
Available upon request

Hardbound ISBN 0-88240-575-6
Softbound ISBN 0-88240-576-4

Alaska Northwest Books®
An imprint of Graphic Arts Center Publishing Company
P.O. Box 10306, Portland, Oregon 97296-0306
503-226-2402; www.gacpc.com

President: Charles M. Hopkins
Associate Publisher: Douglas A. Pfeiffer
Editorial Staff: Timothy W. Frew, Tricia Brown, Kathy Howard, Jean Andrews, Jean Bond-Slaughter
Production Staff: Richard L. Owsiany, Susan Dupere
Editor: Michelle McCann
Designer: Elizabeth Watson

Printed in Hong Kong